EASTERN MADHYA PRADESH

Panna

Bandhavgarh

Satpura

Kanha

Pench

The case of the Missing Tiger Cub

By
Kalpana Subramanian
& Prashant Miranda

GOOD EARTH
A Goodearth Publication

Alone in Bandhavgarh

One spring morning, as the sun painted its golden light over the hilly forests of central India, Rainbow Raghavan stepped outside his cottage. He was in the middle of a jungle resort on the outskirts of Bandhavgarh National Park in Madhya Pradesh.

This is the wild heart of India, where tigers, leopards and elephants roam freely through forests of bamboo and sal. Deer gallop through the grasslands, wading into waterholes and swamps.

This is home to bears, jackals, monkeys, porcupines, snakes, and a host of other creatures. The skies are ruled by birds of every kind. Parakeets, cuckoos, barbets and drongos dart through the air, bursting into song at the break of day.

There is never a quiet day in the forest, and Rainbow Raghavan would soon discover this. At the moment though, he was feeling a little confused. He had never seen animals in the wild!

Ma and Pa were taking him on a safari later this week and he had to admit that it made him a little nervous. Rainbow was an indoor kind of boy. With all this heat, dust, noise and you-name-it, being outdoors terrified him. When he went on school picnics it was always Rainbow Raghavan, not Sturdy Srinivas or Regular Ramya, who would end up with nicks, scrapes, bruises and scratches! Not to mention sneezes...

AAaa...chhHHooOO!

Thank god for handkerchiefs.

Now here he was, at the brink of a wildlife safari.

"Are we really going to see animals outside their cages?" he asked Ma, with a frown, and she replied, "Out in the wild open. And if we get really lucky, a tiger might cross our path!"

What an alarming thought! 'Lucky' was the last word he would have used to describe it. Hmmm, maybe he could fake a stomach ache to avoid any trespassing tigers.

Today, Mr. and Mrs. Raghavan were driving down to Jabalpur to bring Rainbow's grandparents to the cottage for dinner. Till they returned, Zoneboy Mahesh, Rainbow's seventeen-year-old cousin was in charge.

Zoneboy had been playing Space Zombies all night, which had left him looking puffy-eyed and dazed. Rolling down the car window, Mrs. Raghavan called out, "Have fun and don't go wandering about outside the house!"

"Chill, Aunty. I'm not moving and Rainbow never leaves his room anyway. We'll be just fine," replied Zoneboy, as the car shrank into the distance, leaving in its place a cloud of dust.

Back inside, Rainbow's cat, Mini, greeted them. Zoneboy disappeared into his room and returned with a pair of binoculars.

"Are we going to watch birds?" asked Rainbow, excited.

"*You* are, Mister!" said Zoneboy.

"What about you?" asked Rainbow.

"I'm going to fight some Space Zombies, dude. Atom beat my score yesterday. Can't let him get too far!"

"Who's Atom?" asked Rainbow.

"Dunno. Who cares?" mumbled Zoneboy, handing the binoculars to Rainbow who looked a bit foxed. "Just a bot I suppose."

"Can I play too? I'll help you beat Atom!" cried Rainbow.

"Uh oh, I don't think so…this game is only for 15-year-olds and above. You're just eleven, kid!" replied Zoneboy.

"Please! Please!" begged Rainbow.

"Shush, here take these binoculars, they should keep you busy. Adios Amigos!" cried Zoneboy, unmoved. "Don't do anything dumb okay? I'm right here watching you!"

Then he disappeared back into his room, and the door slammed shut. Rainbow sat alone in the kitchen, wondering how his cousin could keep an eye on him through a closed door. Muffled sounds rang out from the game pad as his cousin fired tickle bombs and collected power nuggets in intergalactic space.

How Rainbow wished that he were just four years older. Disappointed, he walked to his own room, alone, except for Mini who glided along by his feet, meowing gently. He bent down to pet her and she purred warmly with delight.

This was Mini's first vacation with the family. The last time the Raghavans had left town, Mini had shredded every cushion and curtain in the house to dust by the time they were back. So, this time there was no question of leaving Mini behind. To Rainbow, Mini was definitely the best cat in the whole world, and she didn't care if he was fifteen or not!

"Oh look Mini!" he exclaimed, pointing at a bird that flew past the window. "It's an Indian Tree Pie!" The bird flew up to a higher branch, allowing him to glimpse its beautiful fan-like tail. If he went upstairs, he would be able to get a better look.

The window in the room above looked out onto the garden and the forest beyond. He was standing at the window trying to spot the Tree Pie, when he noticed a strange movement behind the trees that lined the forest. Mini jumped up next to him, curious as ever. Did she see it too?

As he peered through the binoculars again, he noticed a ripple run through the tall grass that grew between the forest and the cottage. It looked as if something had raced through the grass and moved towards the garden! From the balcony, he would be able to get a better view.

Rainbow knew that he was not supposed to step outside the cottage today, so he hesitated for a moment. But then, a balcony

is neither inside, nor outside, he reasoned with himself. What was the harm? He could run in very quickly if he needed to.

"Just one look, and I'll be back in a jiffy," he promised himself as he opened the balcony door carefully. From there, he scanned the scene once more with great concentration, waiting for a movement to catch his eye, but nothing stirred. Instead, a heavy silence filled the air. Everything was so still, that he could feel his heart beating. It felt as if something was about to happen.

"I should go back inside," he thought, suddenly feeling a bit unnerved. Just then, he heard a loud rustle from not so far away. Panning his binoculars towards the sound, his eyes rested on the garden hedge, which was shaking slightly. Whatever it was, had moved much closer and was probably inside the hedge! He felt something furry touch his leg and nearly jumped out of his skin, only to realise that it was just Mini's tail that had brushed him.

"Oh no, Mini! What are you doing out here?" he whispered anxiously. He had completely forgotten about her, and she had followed him out onto the balcony.

"This is no place for a cat, Mini! Go back inside!" he said firmly, pointing at the door, but Mini just stood there staring hard at the garden hedge below. He would just have to pick her up and bring her in. He scooped her up in his arms, but she deftly shook herself free and leapt onto a branch hanging close to the balcony.

"No, Mini!" he cried as she nimbly made her way down the tree to the garden below. The rustling sound was back, and it was clearly coming from a large bush in the garden, which was visibly shaking. Mini ran towards the bush, and peered into it with all her feline curiosity.

There was something inside that bush and it was too large to be a mouse or a bird.

"Don't go there Mini!" cried Rainbow, not liking the look of things one bit. He grabbed his umbrella and pointed it at the bush.

"Come out! I'm not afraid of you!" he cried out in a challenging tone, brandishing his umbrella like a sword in front of him. The bush grew still, as if in response, but Rainbow knew that it was some kind of trick.

An umbrella is an amazing thing. You can do so many things with it! Those who know Rainbow Raghavan also know that it is his best friend. Next to Mini, of course.

My name is Rainbow Raghavan, and this is my umbrella.
Say what you will, but he is a good fella!
All I have to do is give him a shout
If it so happens that I must step out!

Don't you like stepping out, Rainbow?

Not really. The outdoors, I think, is best seen
from the indoors.
A rule that I just broke, and look, it's landed
me in trouble already

If you do decide to step outdoors
It might serve you well to know
That you should carry an umbrella
Wherever you may go.

Why an umbrella, Rainbow?

The wind can be too breezy
And the sun can be too hot
The rain can be too dripping wet
Believe it, or not!

But Rainbow…

Wait, I can't talk now…
There is something in that bush!

Come sun, rain, wind or snow
I take my umbrella wherever I go!

As Rainbow unfurled his umbrella, attempting to scare the thing in the bush, a young girl leapt out of it, and quick as lightning she drew an arrow at him! Rainbow Raghavan jumped back in fright. The ARROW she held in her hand, was pointed at his HEART.

"Help!" he cried in panic.

She did not move, not by the width of a hair.

"Who are you?" he shouted.

"I'm Arrowgirl Avani. Call me Arrow." Her voice sliced through the air.

She speaks! She could understand him. Perhaps he could reason with her?

Arrowgirl Avani wore the strangest clothes he had ever seen. Her dress was a patchwork of cloth, dried leaves and flowers woven together with odd bits of string. Brightly coloured seeds studded her skirt. Her hair was pinned back with a porcupine quill into a miniature bun, from which hung loose a few tresses amongst which dangled an iridescent feather. Tattoos laced her arms and legs, and the glass bangles on her wrist glinted in the sun. Her fingers gripped the arrow, holding the bowstring taut, but it was her sharp voice that snapped Rainbow out of his stupor.

"Who are you?" she asked.

"I'm Rainbow...Rainbow Raghavan. Please don't point that arrow at me! What do you want?!" he asked desperately.

There was a moment of silence, as their eyes locked, and then her tone softened.

"I…I need your help," she said.

Rainbow's eyes widened. Why should THIS girl need HIS help? She was holding him at arrow-point! He felt a wee bit braver suddenly, and said, "It would certainly help me to help you, if you stopped pointing that arrow in my direction,"

"Are you not scared of me?" she asked somewhat amused.

"Not a bit!" cried Rainbow, lying through his teeth.

Mini had, in the meanwhile, surfaced from the bush and was watching this drama with great interest.

"What's her name?" asked Arrowgirl looking at Mini.

"Her name is Mini," replied Rainbow.

Arrowgirl finally lowered her weapon, and said, gesturing to his umbrella, "Don't point that thing at me again. I don't like it."

"Would never dream of upsetting you!" sighed Rainbow with relief, and asked, "How can I help?"

Taking a deep breath, she whispered, "Help me find Mola!"

"Who is Mola?" asked Rainbow.

"He's a tiger cub," said Arrow.

"You must be joking…" stammered Rainbow.

But Arrow's eyes grew fierce and hypnotic at once.

"Do you think this is funny?" she said slowly.

She doesn't need arrows, with eyes like that, he thought.

"Now wait...look here, I don't know anything about a tiger cub...I cannot help you!" he cried out.

"But you have to help us find him," she said, almost imploring, "Mola is only two-weeks-old and his mother is worried sick!"

Rainbow felt like she was casting a spell on him and he was walking into her trap!

"I can't leave the cottage...my parents...." he protested weakly.

"Of course you can! You'll be back by evening," she said before he could finish his sentence.

"We mustn't go into the forest by ourselves!" he cried out.

"We ab-so-lute-ly must!" she replied firmly.

"No! I am not coming with you. Go away!" cried Rainbow, praying that Zoneboy would not hear them. He would get into trouble for sure. Had he not opened the balcony door, none of this would have happened.

"So, you won't come with me? That is a pity, now, isn't it Mini?"

She said, suddenly turning her attention to the cat.

She knelt down and beckoned Mini towards her, singing a cat-like melody to her in a strange language. Mini started walking towards Arrowgirl as if in a trance.

"Oh Mini, you turncoat, you!" Rainbow cried out as Mini allowed her feline little self to be hypnotised by Arrowgirl. Had Mini missed the bit where Arrowgirl had nearly struck an arrow through his heart? So much for cat loyalty.

Looking at Rainbow's face, Arrow burst out laughing. Her laughter sounded like a flock of parakeets descending on a tree.

"Coming Mini?" said Arrow softly to Mini who swayed her tail coyly in acceptance.

"Leave Mini alone, she's MY cat!" cried Rainbow in horror. Arrowgirl looked at him coolly and said, "YOUR cat? Animals don't belong to anyone. They are free creatures, and they shall roam the earth." With that, she turned around and walked away.

Mini followed her, stopping for a moment to look back and see if Rainbow was coming too. She meowed gently as if to say, "Aren't you coming with us?"

"I can't come Mini! Don't go with her…" he pleaded, but Mini was not going to change her mind. Helplessly he watched as Arrowgirl Avani walked off into the wilderness, with Mini at her heels.

A wave of panic and anger rose inside him. How dare Arrow walk away with Mini like that! Who does she think she is? "I must do something!" he thought, racing back inside. He grabbed a piece of paper and scrawled a note on it as fast as he could.

"Don't wake me up till they come home. I'm sleeping." As he slipped the note under Zoneboy's door, he heard beeping and zapping sounds from inside the room. "He won't be coming out for a while," thought Rainbow as he dashed out of the cottage, closing the door behind him.

The Unfriendly Forest

It was noon and the sun was high up in the sky. As he ran out of the house, Rainbow saw Arrow and Mini disappearing into the tall grass ahead. He ran after them, but they seemed to slip further and further away. The sun was beating down on him and blades of grass tickled his nostrils making him sneeze. He opened his umbrella to shield himself from the blinding glare of the sun and the thorny branches that leapt out at him from every bush.

"Stop!" he shouted as loudly as he could. Arrowgirl stopped and turned to look at him, but then thought the better of it. Turning around, she sprinted like a deer towards the forest, with Mini by her side. Soon, they were mere specks in the distance. Rainbow huffed and puffed after them as they wove their way in and out of the trees. It was like a game of hide and seek, with Arrow and Mini leaping into sight, then disappearing, in the blink of an eye. Dry twigs, branches, rugged pits and stones were like Arrow's forest allies, waiting to trip him at every step. At one point, he lost sight of them altogether.

"Miniiii! Arrow! Where are you?"

He cried out loud but his words were swallowed by an empty silence that caved in around him. A shiver ran up his spine. Suddenly, he realized that he was all alone, in this vast and unknown forest. Maybe not all alone, on second thoughts...

There was a heavy breathing sound behind him.

"Arrow, is that you?" He called out, looking around him anxiously.

But the breathing did not sound human. It was like a sawing sound that grated against his ears. What was this animal lurking in the trees, that he could not see? Whatever it be, he was certainly not going to wait to find out. He ran as fast as his legs could carry him, deeper into the dense forest.

Rambling branches and roots slowed him down, vines entangled him and cobwebs ensnared him! The ground turned slippery with leaves, and he struggled to keep his balance. As he skidded past a tree, his foot tugged at a rope hidden under the leaves, yanking something that let out a snapping metallic sound.

It was a trap, which missed his ankle by a hair, making him leap up in fright and hit a low hanging branch that sent him tumbling down a slope, where he rolled and rolled till the world started spinning around him! He could do nothing but shut his eyes and let go…

When he opened his eyes, he found another pair of eyes looking into his, rather intensely. They were a bit like Mini's but much larger. Mini's eyes were green, but these were like limpid pools of gold. Beautiful, he thought, still reeling from the fall. But as he slowly came to his senses, his heart began to pound. And then it skipped a beat.

Oh yes, there was no mistaking this.

He was looking into the eyes of a Royal Bengal tiger.

"*Panthera tigris tigris*.
Female, eleven years old.
2 metres long and 130 kilograms".
That's not what you want to know...is it?
"Let me tell you her story," said Arrowgirl Avani.

"There was once a tiger called Tina. She gave birth to four little cubs. The news of her cubs had lit up all the vines in the forest. Mitti and Mili were her daughters. Her two sons were Mola and Molu. Their father, Toto, was a very absent-minded chap and never helped Tina take care of the cubs. One day, when he was counting dragonflies in a waterhole, Tina pleaded with him to bring them some food. He got up and ventured out into the forest, but never returned. Tina waited four whole days. There was no sign of him. Toto had forgotten to come back.

"The cubs were just a couple of weeks old and could barely see. They rolled around like little balls of golden fur. Tina was hungry, and hadn't eaten for days. If she did not eat soon, she would grow weak and then who would take care of her cubs?

"So, Tina set out to look for food, hiding her little ones in a cave nearby. But, when she was away... Two men drove into the forest in an old truck and went up to the cave. The tiger cubs started crying out loud, sensing danger, but Tina was far away and could not hear them. I was nearby, though, and I recognized the cries that pierced the air.

"From behind a tree, I spied the two men coming out of the cave with the tiger cubs in a sack. I followed them from a safe distance till I got a chance to slow them down. Then I was able to rescue the cubs and return them to Tina...."

"Then why are you still looking for a missing tiger cub Arrowgirl?" asked Rainbow.

"Because, when I opened the sack, there were only three cubs! I don't know where Mola went. He was just not there!"

At the mention of Mola, Tina's eyes welled up with tears, and she let out an anguished moan. Looking into the eyes of a tiger can transform you forever. Rainbow felt something warm and strong inside him. It rose up like a fire, and he was suddenly bursting with courage like he had never known.

"We will find Mola. I'm going to help you," he said to Arrowgirl.

"I knew you would," she replied with a smile.

Tina looked at both of them, radiating a silent prayer into their hearts.

"How could you have known that?" asked Rainbow, as they walked along.

"Known what?" asked Arrow nonchalantly, carrying Mini in her arms.

"That I would help! I didn't know myself until now," said Rainbow.

"Tiger Spirit told me," said Arrowgirl mysteriously.

"Who's that?"

"He is a special person... he knows things. He said to me that a boy from the city, with a cat, could help me find Mola. That's you, isn't it?" she chuckled.

Rainbow was intrigued, but he had less trouble believing Arrow now.

"Does Tiger Spirit know where Mola is?" he asked.

"Maybe he does, but he speaks in riddles and said he would only tell me if I brought you to him," Arrow said, as they walked through the forest.

"That explains it! What are we waiting for?" asked Rainbow. Mini let out an enthusiastic meow.

"Nothing at all," Arrowgirl replied, grabbing a vine and hauling herself into the air, taking Mini and Rainbow with her.

Rainbow was thrilled to be swinging through the jungle on vines. It was not something he had ever imagined himself doing, but then this was turning out to be a very different kind of day indeed!

Arrow rode the wind like a large bird. Mini was not as excited about being tossed up in the air, and clung tightly to her.

But, Rainbow was loving it. He learnt a few tricks of his own, like how to use his umbrella as a hook and latch on to things. As he rose up in the air, he could feel the wind race past him and the sun kiss his cheeks.

Before long, the forest felt like an old friend that was welcoming him. It was exhilarating to be wild and free. This is what animals must feel like when they are not in cages he thought, as he rode through the forest like one of them.

Tiger Spirit

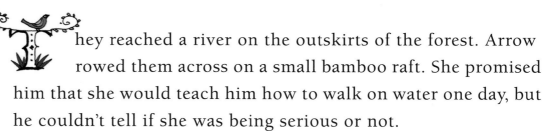

hey reached a river on the outskirts of the forest. Arrow rowed them across on a small bamboo raft. She promised him that she would teach him how to walk on water one day, but he couldn't tell if she was being serious or not.

They made their way towards a village on the other side, where men and women were going about their daily chores. Some were cutting grass or weaving baskets while others were building huts and carrying firewood. A blacksmith was forging tools in his shed.

"The people from this village used to live in the forest before. Now they live here, but they still know everything about it," said Arrow.

"Why don't they live in the forest anymore?" asked Rainbow.

"They had to move, to protect the forest for the sake of the tigers. You know there are very few tigers left now…" said Arrow.

"Where do *you* live?" asked Rainbow, raising an eyebrow.

"Oh me?" she asked, surprised, but before she could answer they were distracted by the delighted squeals of little children who had seen them approaching.

The mud houses had simple geometric shapes painted on them. People's bodies, too, seemed to be painted with curious patterns and symbols. Rainbow's eyes took in every detail as he walked along, enchanted. Finally, they reached a kind of village

square, where people were singing and dancing in a little circle, under a tree, to the beat of drums. A man was spinning round and round in a swirling skirt, holding a bunch of bright feathers in his hand.

Arrowgirl walked up to him and announced, "I have brought him, Tiger Spirit."

The spinning man slowly wound down to a halt and opened his eyes. He had very kind eyes that crinkled up as he smiled. Reaching out with his right hand, he produced a handful of berries from thin air!

"Good! You must be hungry. Eat these delicious berries!" he said, putting them into two little leaf cups. Rainbow and Arrow munched hungrily, while Mini looked on wide-eyed.

"Help us find Mola, Tiger Spirit!" pleaded Arrow.

Tiger Spirit burst out laughing uncontrollably. He was shaking all over! They watched, mesmerised, as he closed his eyes and slowly started to spin again. People started to clap rhythmically and the beat of the drums caught on. The sky began to darken swiftly, and a fire was lit by the village people. Its flickering light danced on Tiger Spirit as he spun at such a speed that he melted into a blurry smoke screen, on which shadowy images started to form!

First the image of a dog appeared, followed by a deer and then an elephant! People cheered aloud each time, and let out animal-like cries. Rainbow felt like he was part of someone else's dream. Mini stayed close to him, not sure of what was happening.

A clear voice floated into the air. It was Tiger Spirit, singing,

"O BROTHER FROM THE JUNGLE
YOU KING OF BEASTS
I INVITE TO JOIN
OUR HUMBLE FEAST

WE ARE PROUD PEOPLE
BUT IN YOU WE TRUST
BECAUSE MAN IS FICKLE
AND WOOD TURNS TO DUST

WE WERE BROTHERS ONCE
BUT WHAT WAS OURS, IS NOW YOURS
WE WAIT FOR DESTINY
TO OPEN NEW DOORS

COME JOIN US MY FRIEND
I CALL FOR YOU NOW
WE MUST SOLVE A RIDDLE
PLEASE TELL US HOW!"

Suddenly, the flickering light grew intense, and a glowing image of a tiger began to burn bright before their eyes! This was what everyone had been waiting for. People started to bow and chant, "Welcome O King!" as they pressed the earth with their palms, the drums building into a frenzy.

"Mola must be found!" Tiger Spirit's cry pierced the air, and suddenly a silence befell them. The smoke screen started to lift and from it emerged Tiger Spirit. The crowd parted as he walked towards them, speaking in riddles.

"WHEN THE GREAT QUEEN LEFT HER PALACE
THREE GOLDEN DROPS WENT MISSING
YET ANOTHER DROP WAS LOST
WHEN THE CROWS
CAME BACK A-FISHING.

THE FOURTH DROP WAS NOT TO BE FOUND
WHEN THE CROWS HAD COME AT FIRST
BUT WHEN THEY RETURNED A SECOND TIME
THIS GOLD DROP QUENCHED
THEIR THIRST.

I SEE THE THIEVING CROWS NOW
HIDING FAR AWAY
IN A LAND THAT MEETS THE OCEAN
WHERE NIGHT IS BRIGHT AS DAY."

"Where is that?" wondered Arrowgirl.

"Somewhere along a coast, but where?!" asked Rainbow, thinking aloud.

Tiger Spirit continued,

"SEVEN DAUGHTERS CAME TOGETHER
MOTHER GAVE THEM HER NAME
SOME GO THERE SEEKING TREASURE
SOME GO THERE SEEKING FAME."

Rainbow's brain was ticking very fast all of a sudden, and he could feel he was on to something.

"A port city...people go there to find money and fame...it all makes sense...but the name?" mumbled Rainbow.

Arrow wished she could read Rainbow's mind. He had a faraway look in his eyes for a moment and then suddenly he snapped his fingers and exclaimed, "I got it! Formed by seven islands and named after their mother...Mumba Devi...it's Mumbai! We have to go there, now!"

"*You* have to go there...I'm not coming!" cried Arrow much to Rainbow's surprise.

"Why not? You made me follow you into the forest and asked me to help you!" he complained to her.

"I don't like leaving the forest, and I get lost in cities," replied Arrow.

"I was more afraid of being lost in a forest, but now I'm not anymore. You, Miss Arrowgirl Avani, are coming with me!"

"But how will we find Mola? We'll get lost!" cried Arrow.

"Maybe you can ask someone for directions there?" suggested Tiger Spirit, looking at Arrowgirl with a smile.

"Who can we ask?" asked Arrow with a frown.

" THERE IS SOMEONE WHO COULD HELP YOU
HE'S A KING WHO HOLDS A CRUTCH
THEY PUT HIM IN A PRISON
BECAUSE HE KNEW TOO MUCH."

"He could only mean the king of the forest…" started Arrow

"Who is in a cage, somewhere in that city!" completed Rainbow, "How do we get to Mumbai in no time, Tiger Spirit?"

"With your umbrella, of course," replied Tiger Spirit in a matter-of-fact voice.

"What do you mean?" cried Rainbow perplexed.

"You tell me," said Tiger Spirit mischievously, "It's yours, is it not?" he said pointing at Rainbow's umbrella.

Rainbow stared at his umbrella so hard, hoping to find a clue, when he suddenly felt it tug at his hand. At once, he knew exactly what he had to do. It was as if the umbrella had spoken to him, as only umbrellas can.

"Hold on!" he said to Arrow, grabbing her hand. Mini jumped onto his shoulder.

Unfurling his umbrella, he shut his eyes and spoke to it silently, willing it to take him to Mumbai. He was concentrating so hard, that his forehead became hot and the umbrella began to glow. He cried out quickly, "Come sun, wind, rain or snow, I take my umbrella wherever I go! Brolly, take me to Mumbai!"

Rainbow and Arrow both felt a gust of wind sweep them up from the ground and carry them into a dreamlike space, where they were encircled by strange whizzing sounds, shooting stars, and odd flashes of light. Maybe they were inside a Space Zombies game, thought Rainbow, and perhaps Zoneboy could see them. A great many things swirled by, but miraculously they crashed into none. Suddenly it all stopped, just as it had started, and they found themselves in a new place! The umbrella which has been glowing like a multicoloured orb was now slowly fading into black again. Mini still looked like she was seeing stars.

"We're in Mumbai," said Rainbow.

The Tiger Who Knew Too Much

They found themselves in front of a sign that read, '**Citizen's Zoo, Mumbai**', and then under it, a smaller one that read, '**Closed today.**'

"I didn't even know Mumbai had a zoo," said Rainbow as they sneaked in through the back gate. He had only been to the zoo in Delhi where he had seen an African rhinoceros called Kalpana.

But this place looked old and forgotten. It felt strange to see such large wild animals in cages that were way too small for them. They saw a poster proclaiming that penguins and cheetahs were soon to be added to the 'impressive collection' of animals. There was even a sign that pointed to a museum of stuffed animals.

"Whatever is that for?" Arrow gave Rainbow an incredulous look, "and why would they want to bring penguins here in the first place?"

Rainbow spotted a sign that read '**Maloom Singh – Tiger Enclosure**'.

"Oh wait!" cried Arrow, "Maloom Singh… I've heard that name before. They used to call him The Tiger Who Knew Too Much!"

"He must have really known something, to have landed up here!" replied Rainbow.

"Everyone wondered, where he had disappeared to! He used to rule the forest!" cried Arrow, excited at the thought of seeing him.

Maloom Singh however, was least concerned by their arrival. He was deeply engrossed in a book on Ranthambore National Park. It had photographs of some of his old hunting pals, but at the moment, it wasn't nostalgia that he felt.

"Oh, I would kill to have this for lunch," he said in a booming voice, pointing to a photo of young sambhar deer, for the benefit of his langoor friend, Flunkie Pandey, who was peeping over his shoulder. Flunkie had his own entrance carved into Maloom Singh's cage, which the zoo-keepers never seemed to notice.

"You certainly would if you could Sir, but don't you think this barasingha would be more your cuppa tea?" said the monkey, pointing to the opposite page, at an image of a handsome young swamp deer.

Maloom guffawed with glee in response. Mini jumped with fright at the sound.

"Err... sorry for the interruption, but we need to speak to you, Maloom Singh!" said Rainbow.

Maloom Singh raised an eyebrow, and without looking up from his book, said to the monkey, "Tut tut, children. In the afternoon...see what the pesky things want, ol' chap. How did they get in here today? I'm not posing for any pictures now."

The monkey bounded around the cage and came closer to them.

"Good afternoon! Flunkie Pandey HMB (Head of Monkey Business), pleased to meet you. Please state your names and the reason for your visit. Maloom Singh speaks to no one, especially on a holiday," he said to them brusquely pulling out his notepad and pen.

“Please listen, Flunkie Pandey HMB! We have to find Mola, the missing tiger cub. We need Maloom’s help,” said Rainbow.

“Well I’m sorry, there is nothing I can do. Please come back tomorrow, we are busy with renovations,” said Flunkie shrugging.

“Renovations?” cried Arrow, incredulously, “Looks like there hasn’t been one here in a hundred years. We’re not going anywhere Mister!”

“Maloom Singh…we know you can hear us!” cried Rainbow, “And we also know that you are just pretending to read your book!”

“Mola the tiger cub is missing! We need your help!” pleaded Arrow. “You are the Tiger Who Knew Too Much, aren’t you?”

That seemed to grab his attention.

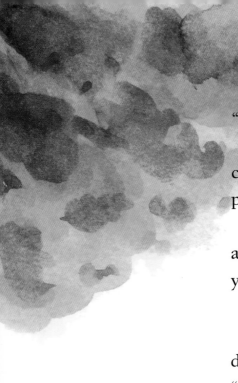

"Hush child!" he said, looking around, and then whispered, "How do you know so much about the Tiger Who Knew Too Much?"

"Well, I've heard of you...animals talk, you know? Tina's cub's gone missing – won't you help us?" cried Arrow in a pressing voice.

"Stop whining, child!" said Maloom, perking up his ears and lowering his reading glasses, suddenly more interested. "Do you mean Tina from the Satpura forests...Bandhavgarh?"

"Yes that's her!" cried Arrow.

"Oh I remember her, she was really something back in the day! Mola's her cub?" he asked, scratching his chin thoughtfully, "Flunkie, do we have anything on him in those files?" he pointed to a cabinet full of files on a shelf. "You know, we get a lot of cases, hard to keep track sometimes!"

Rainbow and Arrow smiled politely, just wishing he would do something.

"Sir, I need to check," said Flunkie pulling out a box labelled **Lost and Found Felines**. One by one, he started flipping through the files calling out the names on the cover, "Jadoo, Meena, Somu..." Mini, whose curiosity preceded her, had slipped into the cage, and was busy poking through the files as well.

The list was long, but there was nothing on Mola.

"That's all we have. No new reports coming in till tomorrow, Sir," Flunkie concluded, putting the files away.

"Tut tut... we can't have Tina in tears, can we now, Flunkie?"

said Maloom, tapping his armrest with his shiny, switchblade like claws.

"No Sir!" cried Flunkie scratching his head.

"We need to activate the network. With your permission, Sir!" he added addressing Maloom Singh with a salute.

"Oh what a fuss, but I suppose it needs to be done," sighed Maloom, giving up on the idea of a quiet afternoon. "Do it then. And put Manju GPS on the case, too."

"Kids, wait outside. We need a few minutes," said Flunkie to them, swinging into action.

"We are outside and would not dream of coming inside, I promise you," said Rainbow.

Arrow tried to suppress her laughter, and said, "He is the funniest tiger I have seen."

"And he," replied Rainbow, as they watched Flunkie get to work, "has got to be the world's most serious monkey!"

The zoo swung to life in an instant. Flunkie passed a message to the sloth bear in the next cage, who passed it on to the wild boar, who in turn passed it on to the python, and so on and so forth, till word had reached every animal in the zoo. When the flamingoes by the waterside got to know, they informed Manju Eagle GPS, who was flying above, doing her daily rounds. Immediately, Manju started scouring every inch of the city for Mola. The city was on high alert. Soon, every animal, bird and insect in the city was looking for the missing tiger cub.

Meanwhile, back at the zoo, Rainbow asked Maloom Singh, "So why do they call you the Tiger Who Knew Too Much?"

"Long story, kiddos. I was the King of the Jungle in my time. Everyone feared me, but they also knew that only I could protect the forest. It was full of riches, and I kept all thieves at bay. I knew every waterhole, beehive, hollow, swamp and den. All the routes that the hunters used, where they laid their snares…there was nothing they could hide from me. But I knew too much, and some people did not like that. Only I stood between them and the great forest. So, one day, they tricked me and I got caught, as

you can see," he said pointing to his bad leg.

"That's terrible Maloom Singh!" cried Arrowgirl.

"What happened then?" asked Rainbow.

"A forest officer rescued me, so I'm here now, till my leg is better. Cases of missing animals keep coming in round the clock, and that keeps me busy. Leopards, vipers, baby elephants, from every forest," Maloom Singh shook his head with disapproval. "I don't take on deer cases though, those are tricky!"

"I'll bet!" said Rainbow, giving Arrowgirl a knowing look and both tried hard not to laugh.

Nothing escapes Manju Eagle's eye, ever. But this time even she couldn't spot anything unusual. Worried, she thought, "I've got to fix these glasses." Putting on her sharpest eye, she continued her search. As she flew over the cargo docks, she spotted two men unloading a suspicious looking sack from a red truck. They took the tiger cub out and put him into a red container on the dock.

"Subject sighted at Dock No.3 at Mumbai Port. Inside a red container marked 'X10', 18° 56.3' N, 72° 45.9'E. Awaiting to load onto cargo ship Blue Olga, leaving for St. Petersburg at 1700 hours," announced Flunkie.

Rainbow cried, "We've got to get to the port, now! It's three o clock already!"

"Come on..." said Arrow, tugging at his arm.

"Kids, run along now! We'll have Manju keep an eye on you," said Maloom.

"And good job, Flunkie ol' chap!" said Maloom to his loyal langoor.

"Thank you! We love you!" cried Rainbow and Arrow.

"Find Mola, and tell Tina, she owes me one. I'll see her when I get out of here," said Maloom with a wink. Rainbow and Arrowgirl waved goodbye to their new friends. Mini slipped out to join them again, as Rainbow unfurled his umbrella and concentrated on the coordinates of the port. Before they knew it, the glowing orb had lifted them into another dimension.

The port was bustling with activity. They spotted the Blue Olga in the distance, and ran towards it. On the dock, opposite the giant ship, were many rows of large metal containers. Manju Eagle was circling a smaller red container, as if to say, "This is it!" Mini scooted towards it and climbed on it, before anyone could stop her. They could hear Mola's squeals coming from inside. Just as they got closer to it, a crane dropped its arm down to pick up the container.

"Stop!" Rainbow called out to the crane operator, but the sound of the machinery was too loud, and the red container was lifted up by the crane, with Mini on it, and Mola inside it! Rainbow quickly hooked his umbrella onto the latch of the container, and he began to rise with it too, legs dangling in the air.

Meanwhile, Arrow scrambled up onto a row of containers close by, and shot an arrow into the air. The arrow jammed the sprocket of the wheel on which rolled the chains, that lifted the container up, bringing it to a jerky halt, mid-air. The container began to tilt to one side, pulled down by its own weight.

Rainbow steadied himself around the corner that he was clinging on to, and wedged open the container door with his umbrella. It flung open, sending objects flying out and hurtling to the ground. Mola the tiger cub slid out with everything else, and landed on his head, making Rainbow nearly lose his balance! His umbrella went flying to the ground.

"Oh noooo!" he screamed as it fell.

The crane operator had come down and several people were now crowding around the scene.

"Look that those crazy children! Stop them!" A man shouted.

Arrow grabbed a dangling chain and swung on it like a vine, to reach the top of the red container.

"Rainbow we have to get away quick, before they take Mola from us!" she cried.

"Call the security!" yelled the crane operator, "There is a tiger up there too!" Some policemen brought a tall ladder and started climbing it to reach them. A security officer, had picked up the umbrella and was examining it carefully.

"Don't touch that!" shouted Rainbow from above. How would they ever get back to the forest without it?

"Manju, grab it!" cried Arrow.

In a second, Manju Eagle swooped down and snatched the umbrella from the guard's hands, flying back to return it to Rainbow.

"Oh thank you!" cried Rainbow, heaving a sigh of relief. Arrow and he were now both standing on top of the container, with Mola and Mini on their shoulders. The policemen were within arm's reach of them, but in the nick of time, they slipped into another dimension, with their magic umbrella, that took them back to the forest.

Mola Returns

It was five o' clock. The bright light of the afternoon sun was now a mellow gold. Little Mola was thrilled to meet Mini, and the two of them bounded alongside. When they reached a little clearing on a hillock, they stopped. It was encircled by bare trees and in front of them lay a great stone sculpture.

"What is that?" asked Rainbow overwhelmed.

"A sleeping god," replied Arrow.

The reclining figure of Vishnu, stretched out before them under the dappled light of the evening sun. He is believed to have dreamt the universe into existence. A seven-headed snake stood guard above him, as he lay, lost in his dream.

Arrow and Rainbow picked Mola up and carefully put him down in front of the figure. They stepped back and watched from a distance as Mola called for his mother. One by one, three little tiger cubs popped their heads out. Tina emerged from behind them like golden cloud. The tears in her eyes glittered like jewels as she gazed at her fourth cub.

The tigress made her way around the statue towards Mola, who could not wait another moment to greet her. He bounded forth on his tiny paws, trying not to lose his balance.

Rubbing her large nose to his, Tina welcomed him with a furry embrace, and he nuzzled up to her, happy to be home.

Mola's brother and sisters greeted him by pouncing on him playfully, and soon they were all tumbling and rolling around the side of the hillock.

Tina's joy was so great, at that moment, that it lit up the earth. Across the river, Tree Spirit sang,

"THE FOURTH GOLDEN DROP
HAS RETURNED TO THE QUEEN
NEVER SUCH JOY
HAS THE FOREST SEEN. "

All the animals of the forest celebrated the return of the missing Tiger cub. The birds sang about it, and the wind whispered it to the

trees. The bare palash trees suddenly burst into blossom, all at once.
The forest glowed like a bed of rubies radiating its light into the skies.

"Your umbrella has just learnt a new trick," said Arrow to
Rainbow.

"Yes indeed!" cried Rainbow as he noticed that it had also turned
a ruby red. "That's camouflage! We must see what else it can do…"

"But really, you must go back now," said Arrow, "It's getting late."

"I thought you would never let me," smiled Rainbow.

"Oh, I'm coming too!" Arrow said.

"But where do you live, Arrow?" asked Rainbow.

"Right next to you. Didn't you notice?" she smiled,
mysteriously.

"At the resort?" he asked, finding it hard to believe her again, but they were already transporting themselves back to the cottage. Arrowgirl Avani bid him goodbye and disappeared around the corner, before he could ask her which cottage she was staying in. Was she really living at the resort? Who was she really?

As he pondered this, he saw the lights come on in Zoneboy's room. Quickly, he slipped into the house with Mini, and crawled into his bed.

"How was your day, Rainbow?" asked Mrs. Raghavan, before she tucked him into bed.

"Fantastic, Ma. I made a new friend," said Rainbow.

"Oh wonderful, who?" asked his mother.

"You'll see!" he said, smiling.

The End

End Notes

Did you know that tigers are the largest felines in the world?

In many cultures they have been admired and worshipped, often seen as protectors of the forests or as gods.

Just within the last hundred years, we have lost 97% of all tigers on the planet. This is mostly due to hunting and the destruction of their habitats.

The Bali, Javan and Caspian tigers are extinct. The remaining subspecies, including the Royal Bengal Tiger, may not survive unless we do something immediately to save them.

Being a top predator, the tiger plays a key role in balancing the ecosystem. When we cut down trees and destroy forests we endanger tigers and the balance of nature, which is important for our own survival.

In order to survive in the wild, they need large areas of peaceful forest, with many large animals to prey on like deer, buffalo and wild pigs to name a few.

Maybe once, people and tigers were able to live in the same forests because there was enough for both. But today, with the number of people going up each day, our needs are more. This causes big problems between people and wildlife. Can we find ways to meet the needs of both people and tigers without harming either?

National parks, reserve forests or wildlife sanctuaries, like Bandhavgarh, are the last refuge for many of our endangered species, not only the tiger.

Bandhavgarh lies among the Vindhya and Satpura mountains in Madhya Pradesh, a central India state that also has other national parks, like Kanha, Satpura, Madhav, Panna and Pench.

Before it became a national park in 1968, Bandhavgarh used to be a hunting ground for kings. It gets its name from a fort on top of a hill, called Bandhavgarh, which means 'Brother's Fort'. The Sheshashayi Vishnu is a famous sculpture in the fort.

There are many tribes in Madhya Pradesh, who have lived for hundreds of years in and around these forests. They continue to keep their ancient customs and wisdom alive in a fast changing world.

The tiger is India's national animal. In 1973, Project Tiger was started in India, to save the species from extinction, but there is much more we need to do, and we can.

What can you do to save tigers? Here are some websites that tell you more:

www.worldwildlife.org
www.truthabouttigers.org
projecttiger.nic.in

A GOODEARTH PUBLICATION
Eicher Goodearth Private Limited
Registered Office: 3rd Floor, Select Citywalk, A-3, District Centre, Saket, New Delhi 110017
www.goodearth.in

First published by Eicher Goodearth Private Limited India 2017
Copyright © Eicher Goodearth Private Limited 2017
Text copyright © Kalpana Subramanian
Illustrations copyright © Prashant Miranda
Design and Layout: Rukminee Guha Thakurta

ISBN 9789380262918

A NOTE ON THE BOOK BY SIMRAN LAL
Dear Parents, Grandparents, Aunts and Uncles and, of course, dear Children,
As a mother of two young ones, I have been inspired to create a series of books that celebrate India's culture, history and geography. Through these books you will enjoy discovering the multi-layered heritage of our country. This one in particular is very close to my heart because it is about celebrating, discovering and understanding our jungles, its animals and our very very precious tiger. Enjoy!

KALPANA SUBRAMANIAN
Kalpana Subramanian is an artist-filmmaker and researcher from India. She was awarded a Fulbright Nehru Academic and Professional Excellence Fellowship in 2015 and the UK Environmental Film Fellowship in 2006. Prashant and Kalpana have collaborated on various creative projects including the The World of Anahi and Vir. This book is in memory of her uncle Gopal, who inspired her to write stories for children.

PRASHANT MIRANDA
Prashant Miranda grew up in Bangalore, studied at the National Institute of Design, India and moved to Canada soon after. He designed children's animated shows for TV in Toronto before moving on to pursue his passions as an artist. He spends his summers in Canada and winters in India, where he travels and documents his life through his watercolour journals, animates films, teaches visual art, illustrates children's books and paints murals.

Printed at Lustra Print Process Pvt. Ltd., New Delhi